Way Down Deep in the Deep Blue Sea

by
Jan Peck

illustrated by
Valeria Petrone

SCHOLASTIC INC.

New York Toronto London Auckland Sydney
Mexico City New Delhi Hong Kong Buenos Aires

My deepest heartfelt thanks to David R. Davis, Cerelle Woods, Melissa Russell, Kathryn Lay, Diane Roberts, BJ Stone, Janet Fick, Debra Deur, Chris Ford, Tom McDermott, Sue Ward, Deborah J. Lightfoot, Trish Holland, Amanda Jenkins, and my editor, Kevin L. Lewis—J. P.

ISBN-13: 978-0-545-00539-5
ISBN-10: 0-545-00539-6

12 11 10 9 8 7 6 5 4 3 2 1   7 8 9 10 11/0

Printed in the U.S.A.   08

This edition first printing, January 2007

Book design by Gregory Stadnyk
The text for this book is set in Fink Heavy.
The illustrations for this book are rendered digitally.

To my Four-Star Critique Group,
and my editor, Kevin L. Lewis—J. P.

For Rosie and Phoebe—V. P.

Way down deep in the deep blue sea,
I'm looking for a treasure
for my mama and me.
I'm so brave,
can't scare me,
way down deep in the deep blue sea.

Way down deep in the deep blue sea,
I spy a sea horse racing by me.
Hello, sea horse.
Giddy-up, sea horse.
See you later, sea horse.

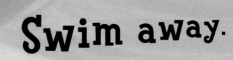

Swim away.

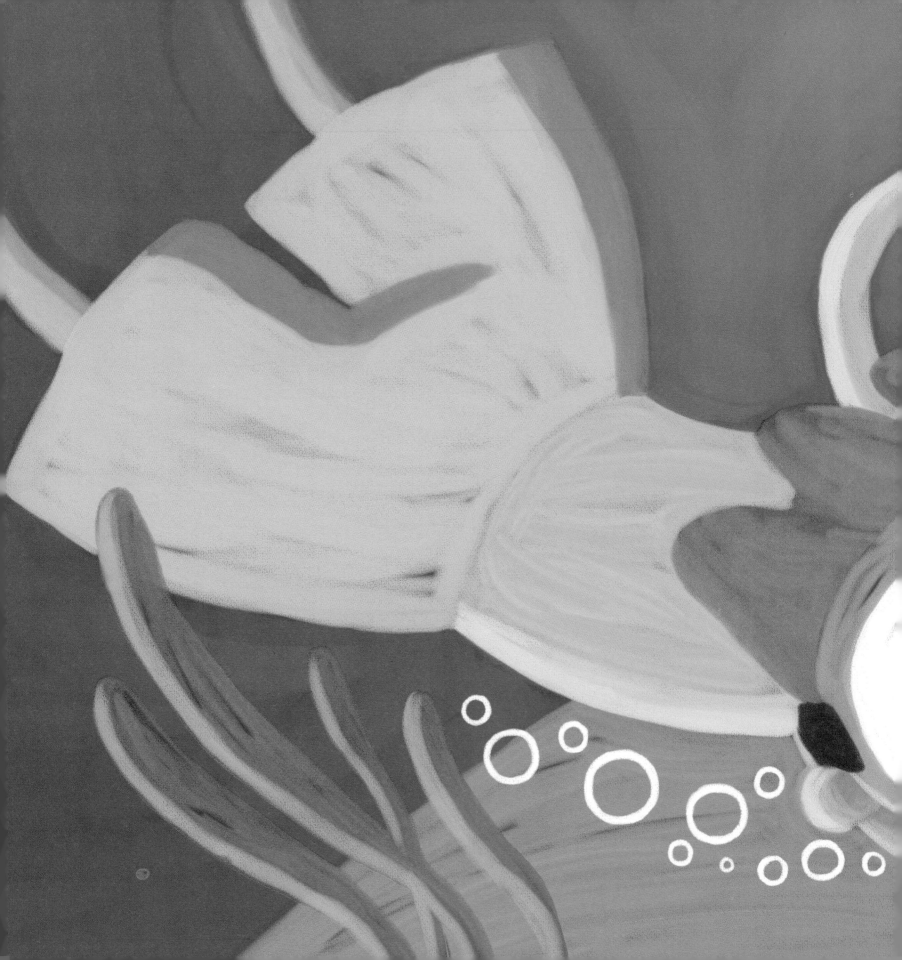

Way down deep in the deep blue sea,
I spy a hermit crab hiding from me.
Hello, crab.
Peek-a-boo, crab.
See you later, crab.

Swim away.

Way down deep in the deep blue sea,
I spy a starfish dancing by me.
Hello, starfish.
Do-si-do, starfish.
See you later, starfish.

Swim away.

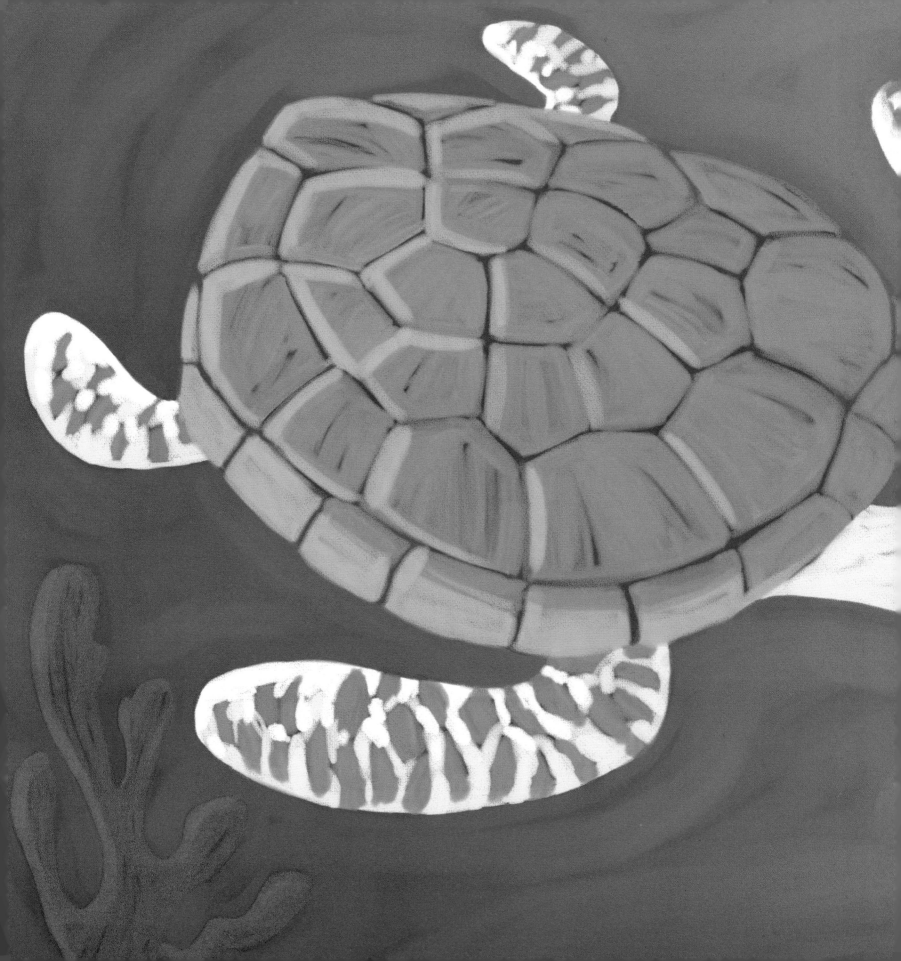

Way down deep in the deep blue sea,
I spy a sea turtle following me.
Hello, turtle.
Tag along, turtle.
See you later, turtle.

Swim away.

Way down deep in the deep blue sea,
I spy an octopus waving at me.
Hello, octopus.
Gimme eight, octopus.
See you later, octopus.

Swim away.

Way down deep in the deep blue sea,
I spy a dolphin diving by me.
Hello, dolphin.
Hitch a ride, dolphin.
See you later, dolphin.

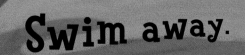

Swim away.

Way down deep in the deep blue sea,
I spy a swordfish fencing with me.
Hello, swordfish.
Touché, swordfish.
See you later, swordfish.

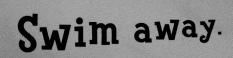

Swim away.

Way down deep in the deep blue sea,
I spy a whale spouting water by me.
Hello, whale.
Sing along, whale.
See you later, whale.

Swim away.

Way down deep in the deep blue sea,
I spy treasure gleaming at me.
Hello, treasure.
Pirate treasure.
Take-along treasure.

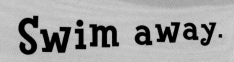

Swim away.

Way down deep in the deep blue sea,
I spy a shark laughing at me!

Good-bye, shark!

Good-bye, whale!
Good-bye, swordfish!
Good-bye, dolphin!

Good-bye, octopus!
Good-bye, turtle!
Good-bye, starfish!
Good-bye, hermit crab!
Good-bye, sea horse!

Up, up, up from the deep blue sea,
I find Mama waiting for me.
Hello, Mama!
Guess what, Mama?
I found treasure in the deep blue sea!